UNICORN ACADEMY
...Where magic happens!

Violet and Twinkle

JULIE
SYKES

illustrated by
LUCY
TRUMAN

nosy
crow

For Mrs MacNish and all at Kincardine-in-Menteith Primary

First published in the UK in 2019 by Nosy Crow Ltd
The Crow's Nest, 14 Baden Place, Crosby Row
London, SE1 1YW, UK

Nosy Crow and associated logos are trademarks and/or registered trademarks of Nosy Crow Ltd

1 3 5 7 9 10 8 6 4 2

A CIP catalogue record for this book will be available from the British Library.

Printed and bound in the UK by Clays Ltd, Elcograf S.p.A.

Papers used by Nosy Crow are made from wood grown in sustainable forests.

ISBN: 978 1 78800 507 4

www.nosycrow.com

CHAPTER ONE

Violet and her unicorn, Twinkle, stood very still as the tiger circled them. It looked straight at Violet, a growl rumbling in its throat. Violet knew it was only Pearl, Matilda's unicorn, using a glamour – an illusion – but it looked just like a real tiger and she couldn't hold back her shriek as the tiger pounced. But then she heard Matilda's giggle and just like that the tiger faded, its paws turning into hooves and its stripy tail growing pink and yellow. Violet grinned as the tiger's last whisker disappeared, leaving Matilda and Pearl in its place.

"Wow! That was brilliant, Matilda! Pearl looked so fierce. I really thought she was going to eat us," said Violet.

Twinkle nodded, adding, "It was very good, even though I could see bits of Pearl's mane showing through the glamour at the end."

Pearl's face fell. Matilda gave her a hug. "Doing a glamour is really hard. It takes a lot of magic to keep it going. I think you did brilliantly, Pearl."

"Me too," said Violet, shooting a look at Twinkle. She knew he didn't mean to be unkind, but sometimes he just said what he thought without realising how it might sound. She did love him, but she found his bluntness quite embarrassing at times. She was the complete opposite to him – she really hated hurting people's feelings.

Nearby, the rest of Diamond dorm were practising doing magic, too. Honey was galloping

Violet and Twinkle

super fast around the frosty garden. Crystal, Rosa's unicorn, was making a snow twister dance across the lawn, and Whisper, Ariana's unicorn, was standing under a tree with a family of timid rabbits playing around his hooves.

When the young unicorns and students first arrived at Unicorn Academy, they were put into pairs by the headteacher, Ms Nettles. They lived at the academy and the students attended classes, where they were taught how to care for their unicorns as well as learning all about beautiful Unicorn Island, where they lived. They also had to discover their unicorn's special magic power and bond with them. While most unicorns and riders achieved this in a year, some needed to stay on for an extra year.

Violet's hands played in Twinkle's thick blue and purple mane. When they finally bonded, a strand of her dark hair would turn the same colour. She bent down and hugged him. "I hope we find your magic soon," she whispered. Violet loved being at the academy, but she didn't want to be the only one of her friends who stayed on for another year.

"Don't worry. We will," Twinkle said confidently.

"I bet I'll have something loads better than Whisper or Crystal's magic."

"Shh!" Violet hushed him as her friends came riding over.

"I don't know about you lot, but I'm ready for hot chocolate," said Rosa.

"Me too, and the unicorns deserve lots of sky berries," said Matilda.

The unicorns whickered happily. Doing magic used a lot of strength and energy, and sky berries were really good for helping them recover.

Diamond dorm rode across the grounds. It was a frosty winter's day and the school buildings were silhouetted against the blue sky, the glass and marble towers sparkling in the pale sunlight.

"It's so strange to think we won't be here after graduation at the end of December," said Ariana.

"Twinkle and I might still be," said Violet. She gave her friends an anxious look. "You'll all write

to me, won't you?"

"No," said Rosa.

Violet's heart lurched.

Rosa grinned. "We're not going to write because you're not going to be here. You and Twinkle will discover his magic and bond very soon. We're all going to graduate together. It'll be perfect!"

The others all smiled and Violet's anxiety faded.

"It would be even more perfect if we could catch the cloaked figure before we graduate," said Freya.

During their year at the academy, the Diamond dorm girls had encountered a mysterious cloaked woman three times. Back in the spring, they had found out that she was taking magic from the Verdant Falls, and in the summer they had discovered she was draining it from the ancient Heart Tree. A month ago, she had tried to frighten them out of an old barn in the school grounds where they had been planning a secret party. It turned out

that the barn hid the entrance to a network of secret tunnels. The mysterious woman had been using the tunnels to move around the school and the grounds unseen, but no one knew why.

"I'm glad the teachers put protection spells on all the entrances to the tunnels so that only teachers and students can use them now," said Violet. Knowing that had made her feel much safer.

"I just wish we could work out who the cloaked figure is," said Freya.

"We've got lots of clues." Rosa started counting them off on her fingers. "One, she's been gathering magic power. Two, she knows a great deal about the school and its hidden tunnels. Three, her unicorn is tall and fast, has a long golden mane, and can cast glamours."

"And four, she wears shoes with a diamond pattern on the soles," added Violet, remembering

some footprints they had found when exploring the secret tunnels.

"Could it be Ms Bramble?" suggested Matilda. "Her knife was found beside the Heart Tree when its magic was being drained. She told us she didn't know how it got there, but she could have been lying."

"Ms Bramble is quite grumpy, but she really seems to care about the island and all the plants in it. I can't imagine her doing anything bad," said Ariana.

"And she doesn't have a unicorn that looks like the cloaked figure's unicorn," Freya pointed out. "None of the teachers do."

"So, it can't be a teacher then," said Violet, feeling relieved. She hated the thought of any of the academy teachers being evil.

"Whoever the cloaked figure is, I bet we haven't seen the last of her," said Rosa. "We must keep

our eyes and ears open. Agreed?"

"Agreed!" they all said in unison.

At the stable block, they were dismounting when Ms Willow, the school nurse, came walking across the grass from the school. She was young and friendly, and the girls really liked her.

"Have you had a nice ride?" she said, smiling.

"A frosty one!" said Violet, her breath coming out in little white puffs.

"Well, don't hang around here too long. You don't want to catch colds." Ms Willow smiled. "Though if you do, I've just brewed a big bottle of special cold-cure medicine, so come and see me! Now, it's time for Daffodil to have some of her health tonic, and I've got some lovely new ribbons to plait into her mane." Ms Willow adored her unicorn, Daffodil, and was always pampering her.

Diamond dorm took their unicorns inside and set about making sure they had thick warm beds

of straw to lie on and bulging hay nets to eat.

As Violet fetched Twinkle some sky berries, she caught sight of Ms Willow braiding Daffodil's pink and yellow mane. The little unicorn's eyes were half closed. Violet felt a pang of envy. She wished Twinkle would let her fuss over him like that, but he didn't like being brushed or having his mane played with. As Ms Willow turned away to fetch some scissors, Daffodil lifted her head and looked at Violet. It was a strange, intense look, almost like she wanted to tell her something. Ms Willow turned back. Seeing Daffodil staring, she glanced round and caught sight of Violet. "Can I help you, dear?"

Violet blushed, feeling like she'd been caught spying on them. "I was just getting some sky berries," she muttered. She hurried on, but the odd expression in Daffodil's eyes stayed with her as she filled Twinkle's bucket in the feed room.

Violet and Twinkle

She glanced back. Ms Willow was now feeding Daffodil a tonic and murmuring in her ear. Daffodil's eyes were half shut again. Violet shook her head. She must have imagined the strange look. She headed back to Twinkle's stable.

"Sky berries!" Twinkle whinnied in delight, plunging his head into the bucket.

"Wait a moment, greedy guts!" Violet laughed. "Let me put them in the manger first."

She emptied them into the manger and he started to gobble them up. "Yum! Thank you!"

Violet sidled closer, wondering if she dared to put an arm round his neck and cuddle him, when he raised his head. "Listen, Violet," he declared, through a mouthful of berries. "We really need to find my magic and bond as soon as possible. I think we should spend more time together."

Violet's heart lifted. "Yes, I could come to the stable more and brush you and plait ribbons in your mane and—"

"Boring!" Twinkle snorted. "No, I was thinking we could go on some night-time rides, galloping under the stars. Just you and me." He looked eagerly at her. "It's a great idea, isn't it?"

He looked so pleased with himself that Violet didn't have the heart to tell him that she would really rather spend time in the stable, cuddling him and talking. She nodded. "OK, let's."

"I knew you'd love my idea," Twinkle declared happily. "I'm sure it'll help us bond. Shall we

go tonight?"

"I can't. There's an inter-dorm quiz tonight," said Violet. "But we could go tomorrow."

"Tomorrow it is then!" Twinkle gave her a quick nuzzle before plunging his nose into the manger again.

Violet gave a little sigh. She loved the fact that Twinkle was full of ideas, but she wished he would occasionally listen to what she wanted to do. Still, maybe going on night-time rides really would help them to bond. *Oh, I hope so*, Violet thought. *I really want to be able to graduate with our friends!*

CHAPTER TWO

The quiz was great fun but very competitive. At the last question, Diamond and Ruby dorms were tying for the lead. Ms Rosemary smiled round at the sea of tense faces as she asked, "Which bird has yellow, orange and red feathers? Isla?" she added, as Isla from Ruby dorm stuck her hand in the air.

"The sun carrot!" shouted Isla. "Noooooo! I mean the sun. . ."

"Wrong!" said Ms Rosemary, barely making her voice heard over the howls of laughter. "Sorry, Isla, I have to take your first answer. Anyone else?"

"The sun parrot," said Matilda. "Yay! Diamond

girls win!" She fell on her friends, pulling them in for a group hug. But when Ms Rosemary gave Diamond dorm their prize – a huge bag of sweets – Matilda shared them out with the girls from Ruby dorm, saying, "Because Isla helped us to win and made us laugh."

Munching her sweets and looking around at all the laughing, chattering students, Violet felt a tingly rush of happiness. She was so lucky to be at Unicorn Academy. If she could just bond with Twinkle and find out his magic, everything really would be perfect!

The following morning, everyone crowded into the stable block for a lesson on bonding taught by Ms Rosemary, the Care of Unicorns teacher. It was a cold day and Violet was glad of her thick woolly socks and snuggly blue Unicorn Academy hoodie. She listened eagerly to Ms Rosemary, wanting to learn all she could.

"Any questions?" Ms Rosemary finally asked, when she had finished her talk.

Violet hesitated. She had something to ask, but what if her question was silly? She started to raise her hand, but then changed her mind. However, Ms Rosemary had noticed.

"Violet, you look like you have a question," she said with a smile. "Don't worry. You can ask anything."

"Er, I just wondered if there's ever been a rider and their unicorn who haven't bonded?" Violet's face warmed as all eyes turned her way.

"Well, that's so rare it almost never happens. Riders and their unicorns nearly always bond within two years."

Violet felt relieved.

Isla put up her hand. "Can someone force a unicorn to bond with them? Last year, a unicorn was stolen from near my home. My mum said she

didn't understand why someone would do that because no unicorn would work with someone else when they'd already bonded. But what if the stolen unicorn was forced to bond again?"

"That would be awful!" said Matilda, stroking Pearl's nose.

"I couldn't bear it," said Rosa, hugging Crystal.

"I've never heard of any unicorn being stolen," said Valentina, who was also from Ruby dorm. She gave Isla a scornful look. "I bet it's just a rumour that someone started to scare people."

"Actually, Valentina, it's not a rumour – it's true," said Ms Rosemary. "It was a unicorn called Prancer and it was a terrible business." She shook her head. "I knew Prancer well. Her partner, Lacey, was at the school here when I was a pupil and we were friends. Prancer was a splendid unicorn with quite the longest mane I've ever seen. It was pure gold. She was very powerful too,

a spell weaver – that's a unicorn who can put their magic into any spell."

"She can't have been very powerful if she allowed herself to be stolen," said Twinkle, with an unimpressed snort. "No one could steal me away from Violet. I wouldn't let them."

Violet blushed at his rudeness.

"Well, I'm sure you'd put up a good fight, Twinkle," said Ms Rosemary kindly. "But if a

unicorn as powerful as Prancer was taken, then no unicorn is safe. However, here at Unicorn Academy, you will be fine, so please don't worry. And, in answer to your original question, Isla – no, no one can force a unicorn to bond with them. It simply isn't possible. A unicorn might be forced to work for someone through dark magic, but not to bond. Bonding only happens when the time is right and a rider and their unicorn become true friends." Ms Rosemary beamed at the class. "Right then, let's finish off here and go out for a ride!"

"That was a really interesting lesson," Violet said to Freya, as they headed to their unicorns' stables.

"Hmm?" Freya looked miles away.

"What's up?" asked Violet.

"It's just the name of that unicorn who was stolen – Prancer – I'm sure I've heard it before,"

said Freya.

"Me too!" exclaimed Matilda, overhearing.

"I haven't," said Violet, puzzled.

"So, where did we hear it?" said Freya, frowning at Matilda.

Matilda shrugged. "I don't know."

"I thought Ms Rosemary would never stop talking," said Twinkle to Violet, when she went into his stable. "She went on and on, didn't she?"

Violet had enjoyed the lesson but she didn't want to disagree with him. "She did a bit."

"It'll be fun going out now with everyone, but we are still going out for a ride on our own tonight, aren't we?" Twinkle nudged her with his nose.

Violet nodded. "I'll come here straight after dinner."

Twinkle snorted happily. "Yay! I can't wait!"

All day, Violet kept thinking about everything

Violet and Twinkle

Ms Rosemary had told them. Bonding happened when a rider and their unicorn became true friends, so why hadn't she and Twinkle bonded yet? She was sure they were already true friends. They loved each other and they never argued – she always just let him have his way. It didn't make sense.

"Is anyone up for a game of Hungry Unicorns?" Ariana asked before dinner. Amidst a chorus of yeses, Ariana went to the cupboard to get the board game out. But as she opened the door, a pile of drawings fell out. "Matilda!" she said in exasperation. "Are these yours?"

"Yep. Sorry. I chucked them in there the other day when we had to tidy the dorm, and then forgot about them," said Matilda, who loved to draw and paint.

"What a surprise!" Ariana rolled her eyes. She was super neat and tidy and Matilda's messiness

drove her crazy. She helped Matilda to gather up the drawings.

Suddenly Matilda stopped, her mouth falling open as she held up a sketch. "Prancer! I thought I knew the name!" She swung round to Freya. "There's a picture of a unicorn called Prancer hanging in the secret tower room above our dorm. I copied it when we were up there working on your unicorn robot before the party!"

"Let me see." Rosa took the paper from Matilda as everyone gathered around. It was a drawing of a magnificent unicorn with a long golden mane.

"Do you think it's the same Prancer who was stolen?" asked Freya.

"It could be," said Ariana. "It looks just like the unicorn Ms Rosemary described."

"Let's go and see the picture," said Rosa.

Everyone rushed for the door, with Rosa leading the way up the spiral staircase, past their

dormitory and on to the secret room. They hadn't been there since the party a month ago.

Reaching the small landing with the huge cupboard, Rosa beckoned Freya forward. "It's your room really, Freya. You discovered it, so you open the door."

Hidden on the back wall of the cupboard was a lever. Freya pulled it and, with a muffled creak, the whole wall spun round. Violet and the others followed Freya through the cupboard and into the secret room beyond.

Shelves lined the curved walls and there was a large desk to one side, but the girls headed straight for a painting hanging on the wall over the fireplace. It was a picture of a tall unicorn with a flowing golden mane. The name "Prancer" was written beneath it.

Matilda caught her breath. "You know something? She looks just like the unicorn the

mysterious woman rides. Do you think that woman stole her?"

Freya nodded. "I bet she did. The cloaked figure's unicorn can gallop fast, appear and disappear and cast glamours – all things a spell

weaver can do."

Rosa paced around the tower room. "I wonder why there's a picture of her in here."

"Maybe the cloaked figure put it in this room for some reason?" Matilda suggested. "She tried to scare Freya and me away from here by making ghostly sounds when we were working on the robot. Maybe she did that because there was something she wanted to use the room for."

"I bet you're right, Matilda!" Freya said excitedly. "And you know what? I think she's been in here since I was last here! Those jars of herbs on the shelves were full before, but now they're more than half empty. And those are new." Freya marched over to the desk and pointed to some wiggly black marks scorched into the surface. "There was only one scorch mark before. I'm sure of it."

Ariana squeaked. "And look at that, everyone!"

She pointed to a faint diamond-patterned footprint in the dust by the fireplace. "It's the same as the footprints we found down in the tunnels!"

"The cloaked figure must have been using this room," said Rosa in excitement.

"Wait!" Violet didn't like disagreeing with her friends, but she'd had an important thought. "What about the spells the teachers put on the entrances to the tunnels? The cloaked figure shouldn't be able to use them to come up here anymore."

There was a moment's silence as they all thought about it.

"True—" Freya began.

"Unless," interrupted Rosa. "The cloaked figure is someone who's part of the school, so the spells don't work on her!"

"A teacher?" breathed Matilda.

"But we've already said none of the teachers' unicorns look like Prancer," Violet pointed out.

"So, maybe it's a student?" Freya gasped. "Quite a few of the students' unicorns have golden manes. Golden Briar does – Valentina's unicorn."

"I don't know," said Rosa. "But I think we need to do some serious investigating."

"I think what we need to do is tell Ms Nettles what we've found," said Ariana.

"Me too," said Violet.

"Not yet," said Rosa quickly. "I think we should wait and see if we can find out anything more."

"I'm with Rosa," said Matilda, her eyes shining. "Let's try to solve the mystery ourselves. Freya, you agree with us, don't you?"

Freya hesitated, but then nodded. "I guess so. If we all stick together, we should be safe. We

may be able to find out more than the teachers, because the cloaked figure won't be expecting us to be looking for her."

"It'll be fun," Rosa declared. "Come on, Violet. You know you want to solve the mystery!"

Ariana glanced at Violet as if to say, *if you don't give in, then I won't either.* Violet felt torn. She wanted to tell Ms Nettles, but she didn't want to upset the others or make them cross with her. Sending Ariana an apologetic smile, Violet caved in.

"OK," she said reluctantly.

"Yay!" Rosa shot Ariana a triumphant grin. "That's four against one."

Ariana sighed. "All right then, we don't tell Ms Nettles yet. But we have to be really careful."

"We will be!" Rosa promised her.

As they all fist-bumped, the pencil that Matilda usually carried behind her ear fell to the ground and rolled under the desk. Crouching down to

pick it up, she frowned. "What's this?" She held up a scrap of silvery-grey fabric with burnt edges.

"It's just an old piece of material," said Freya, examining it.

"It might be a clue," said Violet, peering over Freya's shoulder. The fabric was shimmery and very soft.

The sound of a bell ringing faintly in the distance made them all jump.

"It's dinner time," said Ariana. "We'd better go downstairs."

Rosa grinned. "Then after dinner we can think of a plan. We're going to solve this mystery – I just know we are!"

CHAPTER THREE

"Planning time!" announced Rosa happily, when they all gathered in Diamond Dorm after dinner.

Violet longed to stay, but she had to keep her promise to Twinkle. "I'm sorry, but I've got to go to the stables."

"Why?" Matilda asked.

"Twinkle wants us to spend time together – he thinks it might help us bond," she explained.

Her friends nodded. "Then you should go," said Freya.

"Definitely," said Matilda.

Violet put on her coat and gloves and slipped

out of the dorm. It was very cold outside. Her feet crunched on the frosty grass. Glancing up at the sky, she hoped it wouldn't snow.

There was a rustle in some nearby bushes. A shiver ran down her spine. What if the cloaked figure was also out in the garden? Feeling uneasy, she broke into a run and sprinted to the stable block. It was a relief to dive inside. As she stood breathing in the sweet smell of hay and letting her heart slow down, she heard a murmur of voices from Twinkle's stall. Who was he talking to? Violet went closer and listened.

"Try not to worry about it," Daffodil was saying in a kindly voice. "You will find your magic soon and bond with Violet, I know it."

Violet smiled at Daffodil's words of encouragement. The little unicorn was just like Ms Willow, so kind.

"It's hard not to worry," Twinkle admitted. "I

don't want to let Violet down, Daffodil."

Violet felt a rush of surprise. She hadn't thought Twinkle worried about things like that.

"You won't let her down," said Daffodil. "You'll bond soon and then you'll be together forever."

Violet caught a note of wistfulness in her voice but Twinkle didn't seem to notice.

"I wish I could do something to make it happen."

"This starlight ride is an excellent idea. The more time you spend together the better," said Daffodil. "Have fun. You only get one special partner, Twinkle. Make the most of her." She left his stall and went slowly back to her own. Violet watched her with a frown. Daffodil looked upset. But why?

She waited until Daffodil went into her stall and then she stepped out of the shadows, pretending that she'd just arrived. "Hi, Twinkle. What's been happening?"

"Nothing much," said Twinkle quickly.

Violet was a little surprised that he didn't mention his talk with Daffodil.

"Let's get going," he said. "It's a cold night. It might even snow!"

They left the stable and rode over to the stream at the bottom of the meadow, where they stopped and watched the dark water flowing by.

The starlight made the water glitter. In a nearby tree, an owl hooted softly. Twinkle sighed happily. "I love night-time, when the stars are shining," he said. "It makes me feel all tingly. Do you like it too?"

"Oh, yes," agreed Violet.

It was lovely being there with Twinkle in the starlight, but she could feel the cold seeping into her fingers and toes despite her thick gloves and socks. She also kept thinking about his conversation with Daffodil. Why hadn't he mentioned it?

"Twinkle. . ."

"You're shivering!"

They had spoken at the same time.

"You first," said Violet.

"I can feel you're cold," he said, sounding concerned. "Put your hands in my mane to warm up."

Violet sunk her hands into Twinkle's long mane

and immediately felt warmer, both inside and out. "That's better," she said, gazing up at the sparkling sky.

"Look, a shooting star!" said Twinkle. "Make a wish, Violet!"

They both watched the star arching over them.

"Do you think we wished the same thing?" Twinkle asked.

Violet smiled. "I think we might have done."

"Now, what were you going to say?" asked Twinkle.

Violet had wanted to ask about Daffodil's visit, but she didn't feel like spoiling the special moment. "It was nothing important. This is so nice – just being here with you. The two of us together."

Twinkle stamped a hoof. "It really is, but even I'm getting cold now."

A pink spark caught Violet's eye. Had that just flown up from Twinkle's hoof? Hope bubbled

inside her as she breathed in a faint scent of burnt sugar – the smell of magic. "Twinkle, did you see that?"

"See what?" he asked.

Violet hesitated. The spark had vanished now and she didn't want to get his hopes up just in case she'd imagined it. "Nothing. Should we walk on a little way and try to warm up?"

"Cantering will do that better than walking!" said Twinkle.

They cantered on, leaving the meadow behind them and entering the copse of trees beyond it. A chill wind picked up and Violet pulled her hood over her head, grateful for its softness and warmth. She stroked Twinkle's neck and let him pick his way through the trees, slowing to watch a family of storm raccoons frolicking in a clearing. Violet was enjoying herself so much that she hardly noticed the first few flakes of snow. It

was only when they came out of the trees that she realised it was snowing quite heavily. "It's a blizzard, Twinkle!" It was falling so thickly, she couldn't even see the school.

"Should we go back?" Twinkle asked.

Violet shivered as the flakes landed on her coat. "I think we'd better."

Twinkle set off into the snow storm. The flakes swirled heavily, covering them both with a cold white layer. Anxiety spiralled through Violet. What if they got lost? What if they froze out here? She squeaked, her hands clutching at Twinkle's neck as he stumbled over a stone.

"Don't worry,

Violet. We're going to be fine. I'll look after you, I promise," declared Twinkle, stamping his feet as he strode through the snow.

Violet felt her panic start to fade and a feeling of confidence fill her. Nothing bad was going to happen, not when Twinkle was with her. She sat up a bit taller and blinked. Weird. It was still snowing, only not on them any more. It was almost like they had a huge umbrella overhead, protecting them. Violet caught a whiff of burnt sugar, and Twinkle gave a surprised snort. "What's going on?" she said. "Twinkle—"

She broke off as a flurry of snowflakes landed on her head, making her gasp out loud. She must have imagined it. Snowflakes were certainly landing on her again now! But, she realised, she could see the lights of the school ahead. "We're almost back, Twinkle!" she said in relief.

"I'll have us back safe and sound in no time at

all," he said, breaking into a canter.

"Where are you going? This isn't the way to the stables," Violet said, as Twinkle veered away from the stable block and headed towards the school.

"I'm going to take you back first." Twinkle cantered up to the academy and stopped at the door. "You go in and get warm."

"No," said Violet, through chattering teeth. "Take me back to the stables so I can brush the snow from your coat. You'll catch a chill if you sleep when you're wet."

Twinkle chuckled. "I'll be fine. I'll roll in my straw bed to get dry. Now stop arguing or I'll carry you all the way up to your dorm!"

"Twinkle!" Violet groaned, but she had to admit that for once she didn't mind him taking control. "Are you sure?"

"Absolutely," he said. "You mean everything to me, Violet. Keeping you safe is the most important

thing in the world."

"Really?" Violet slid from his back and threw her arms round him.

Twinkle let her hug him for once. "Yes, really," he said, nuzzling her. "Now go!"

"But how will I know you get back safely?" she said anxiously. "That's just as important to me."

"Watch me from inside, and don't worry, I'll be back in my warm stable in two shakes of a unicorn's tail."

Violet kissed him. "All right then. Night, Twinkle."

She ran inside and watched from a window as he cantered back to the stable block. The starlight ride had been far more adventurous than she had expected! Suddenly she remembered the pink spark she'd seen when they'd been standing in the meadow, looking at the stars – she was sure she had seen it. Had that been a hint that Twinkle's magic was going to appear soon? Feeling a flutter of excitement and hope, she ran upstairs to the dorm.

CHAPTER
FOUR

Violet's friends were all very relieved to see her. "We've been worried about you," said Ariana, hurrying over. "We thought you might be lost in the snow."

"We were, but Twinkle was amazing." Violet sat on her bed and pulled her thick duvet around her. She told the others how Twinkle had brought them safely back through the snow. She decided not to tell them about the pink spark, just in case she'd imagined it.

Matilda hugged her. "Well, I'm very glad you're back."

Violet smiled. Her friends were the best!

"So, do you want to hear what we've decided to do about the cloaked figure?" said Rosa, her eyes shining. She jumped on to Violet's bed. "Tomorrow night, we're going to sneak into the teachers' quarters and spy on them!"

Matilda grinned, but Freya frowned. "I really don't think it's a good idea."

"Freya and Ariana have said they won't come, but you will, won't you, Violet?" said Rosa.

"Um. . ."

"Pleeeeeeease!" said Matilda.

Violet really didn't want to. "Well. . ."

"We won't take no for an answer," said Rosa firmly.

"Oh, all right then," said Violet, giving in. Rosa and Matilda beamed.

"Awesome! So, tomorrow night, our spying mission begins!" Rosa declared.

Violet was tired the next day. In the Healing with Herbs lesson, grumpy Ms Bramble shouted at her twice for yawning. Violet was extremely relieved when Ms Bramble ended the lesson early and sent them for lunch. After a warming bowl of soup with hot crusty bread, Violet and the other Diamond dorm girls went to the stables to visit their unicorns. Shouts of laughter greeted them across the yard. They hurried inside and found Miki, Himmat and the boys from Topaz dorm pretending to duel with hockey sticks.

"What's going on?" asked Rosa.

"Jake's fighting us! We tricked him. He's never played unicorn hockey before so we told him the sticks were used to pull riders from their unicorns." Miki could hardly speak for laughing.

Himmat doubled over. "And once you'd caught a rider, you used the stick to hook him up by his

hoodie on a fence post."

"I knew you were joking," said Jake, waving his hockey stick.

"Did not!" yelled Miki and Himmat.

Rosa burst out laughing too. "That's mean. Genius, but still mean!"

"We know!"

When everyone had eventually calmed down, Freya said, "Honey loves unicorn hockey. Who's up for a game in the snow, Diamond dorm against

Topaz?"

"I'm in," said Ariana. "I'm hopeless at hockey, but Whisper loves anything like that."

Twinkle looked out of his stable. "Hockey's boring," he said loudly.

Violet cringed at his rudeness, but Himmat just grinned. "Oh, hockey's boring, is it? Obviously you've never played with us. Am I right, Miki?"

"Yeah," said Miki. "No one gets bored the way we play! Come on, Violet. You'll join in, won't you?" He went to hand Violet a hockey stick, but Twinkle stepped out of the stable and stood in his way.

"Violet doesn't want to play hockey."

"Wow, Violet! You said that without even moving your mouth," joked Miki. He wiggled a hockey stick at her, trying to pass it around Twinkle. "Go on, give it a try!"

"I . . . Um. . . Well. . ." Violet's cheeks burned

as everyone turned to look at her. She really wanted to play, but she didn't want to fall out with Twinkle, especially after their closeness last night.

"Violet?" said Himmat.

Violet didn't know what to do. "Sorry," she gasped suddenly. "I've got a headache. I'm going back to the dorm." She hurried away, sure that everyone would guess she was just chickening out of making a choice. Why couldn't Twinkle just ask what she wanted to do for a change? Once she was outside the stables, she ran all the way to the academy. She yanked the door open and almost bumped into Isla, who was on her way out.

"Whoops! Sorry!" said Isla. She frowned. "Hey, are you OK, Violet? Has someone upset you?"

"I'm fine," muttered Violet.

Isla looked doubtful. "You don't look fine." She pulled Violet inside and over to a large window seat. "What's up?"

47

Isla sounded so sincere that Violet couldn't stop herself. She found herself blurting out what had happened and once she'd started, she couldn't stop. Soon Isla knew all about her worries and concerns about Twinkle. "I don't think he means to be rude," Violet finished. "But I can't help thinking that we'll never bond if he doesn't listen to me or think about what I want."

Isla gave Violet's arm a sympathetic squeeze. "Twinkle hasn't always been this bad, has he?" she said thoughtfully. "He's the last unicorn in your dorm not to have found his magic or bonded. I bet he's worried and that's why he's bossier than normal. Maybe you should try talking to him about what you want when he starts making decisions for both of you."

Violet squirmed. "He'll get upset. I'd rather just not say anything and make him happy."

"But that isn't making *you* happy," Isla pointed out.

Violet swallowed and voiced her biggest fear. "Oh, Isla, what if we don't ever bond?"

"Of course you will! I haven't bonded with Buttercup yet, either, but it'll happen. Remember what Ms Rosemary said in the lesson? It's very rare for a rider and unicorn not to bond." Isla took Violet's hand. "We've got to keep believing that."

Violet nodded and the two girls shared a hopeful smile.

CHAPTER FIVE

To Violet's relief, when everyone returned from unicorn hockey, rosy-cheeked and chattering happily, they didn't mention the scene in the stables with Twinkle. "So, tonight!" Rosa said, bouncing up to Violet. "We'll start snooping after dinner. OK?"

"OK," said Violet reluctantly.

"You don't have to go, Violet," said Ariana. "You can stay with me and Freya."

"Nope, Violet's coming with us," declared Rosa. "And that's that!"

Before bedtime, Violet found herself shivering

in a dark corridor in the teachers' quarters, wearing her dressing gown and fluffy polar bear slippers as she crept behind Rosa and Matilda. Every cell in her body was wishing she was back in the dorm with Freya and Ariana.

"What exactly are we looking for, Rosa?" asked Matilda. She swung her torch wildly, sending a dancing beam of light along the ceiling.

"Shoes!" announced Rosa. "We're going to see if any of the teachers' shoes have a diamond pattern on the sole."

Violet really didn't want to sneak into the teachers' rooms. "How about we look in the staff cloakroom?" she suggested.

Rosa's eyes sparkled in the torchlight. "Ooh, yes! Good plan. The teachers will all be in the staff common room after dinner."

The staff cloakroom was near the back door. It was lined with pegs with shoe racks underneath.

"Look at all these shoes," Matilda whispered as they went inside and shut the door behind them. "It's going to take ages to check them."

The girls set to work, using their torches to see the patterns on the soles of the riding boots, wellies and shoes. Rosa and Matilda were soon giggling.

"Look at this!" said Matilda, pulling a pink, yellow and very fluffy sock out of a boot and carefully holding it up. "Whose is it?"

"Ms Bramble's?" Rosa suggested innocently, causing Matilda to snort loudly.

Matilda dropped the thing back into the boot and then pulled out a pair of old green socks from some wellies. "Eew! Smelly!" she squealed, dropping them. Clutching on to Rosa, she rocked with laughter.

Violet's heart was thumping and it beat even faster when she heard a creak outside. "Shhh," she said. "What's that?"

But Rosa and Matilda were giggling too hard and didn't hear her.

"Quiet!" Violet hissed.

The door opened and the light snapped on. Matilda squeaked and Violet's torch clattered to the floor.

"Girls!" Ms Willow stood in the doorway, dressed in a thick scarf and outdoor coat and holding an empty bottle of Daffodil's tonic. "What are you

doing in here?"

Violet felt like crying. They were going to get into so much trouble. She'd known this was a bad idea.

"We. . . Um. . ." For once even Rosa was lost for words.

Ms Willow looked at them for a

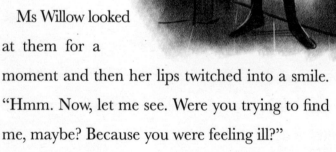

moment and then her lips twitched into a smile. "Hmm. Now, let me see. Were you trying to find me, maybe? Because you were feeling ill?"

Violet blinked. It sounded almost like Ms Willow was trying to give them a way out – an excuse for being there.

"Yes," said Matilda, her eyes widening. "We felt unwell."

Rosa nodded vigorously. "We thought. . . We thought we might have colds coming on."

"Well, in that case, I'll overlook you all being here, provided it doesn't happen again. Now, why don't you hurry along to bed and I'll bring you some of my cold-cure medicine. Unless you're already feeling a bit better?" Ms Willow's eyes twinkled.

"Actually, I think we'll be fine," Rosa gasped.

Violet couldn't believe it. Thank goodness lovely Ms Willow had found them! If Ms Brambles or Ms Rivers had discovered them, they would certainly have been marched straight to Ms Nettles.

Ms Willow ushered the girls from the cloakroom. "Go back to your dorm, girls. If I hear any noise, I'll be up with that cold-cure medicine in the

stamp of a unicorn's hoof. Understand?"

"We understand!" they all answered as they scurried away.

"Phew! That was close!" said Rosa, when they'd turned a corner.

Matilda blew out a long breath. "Hurrah for Ms Willow! She really is the best."

Violet nodded, feeling cross with herself. She'd known all along that Rosa's spying mission was a bad idea. So why had she gone along with it? *If anyone asks me to do something I don't want to again, I'm definitely going to say no*, she decided firmly, *even if it's Twinkle!* But would she really argue with him? Not wanting to think about it, Violet squashed her thoughts down and quickly ran upstairs with the others.

CHAPTER SIX

"Get up, sleepy." Violet woke to find Ariana gently shaking her by the shoulder.

Violet sat up slowly, blinking the sleep from her eyes. Hot shame flooded through her as she remembered the spying and being caught by Ms Willow. She glanced over at Rosa and Matilda. Neither of them seemed bothered by the experience. In fact, Rosa was gleefully re-enacting the moment in the cloakroom when they'd been caught.

"It was so funny," she said to the others. "You should have seen our faces!"

"Lucky it was only Ms Willow," said Freya.

Rosa nodded. "She's the best. Well, I guess that means we can't do any more night-time spying for the moment."

"Good," said Ariana. "So, does that mean we can tell Ms Nettles?"

"Just a few more days," begged Rosa. "And if we haven't found anything else out by then, we can tell her. I promise!"

At lunchtime, Violet slipped away from her friends and went to the stables to see Twinkle. He was talking to Daffodil and looked surprised to see her.

"Do we have a lesson now?" he asked. "I thought it was lunchtime."

"It is," said Violet. "I just thought I'd spend some time with you. I could plait some ribbons into your mane? Daffodil's ribbons look really pretty."

A strange expression crossed Daffodil's face but was gone so quickly Violet decided she must have imagined it.

"Twinkle was just telling me about your adventure the other night," said Daffodil. "It sounds very exciting."

Twinkle snorted. "It was! Why don't we go out for a ride now, Violet? The snow's gone."

Violet took a breath and lifted her chin. "I want to stay in and plait your mane."

Twinkle looked surprised. "But I want to go out."

"Twinkle, maybe you should do what Violet wants to do for a change," suggested Daffodil. "You always seem to make the decisions for the pair of you."

"Do I?" Twinkle was surprised. "Oh, all right then, we can stay in and you can put ribbons in my mane, Violet."

Violet blinked. She'd got what she wanted without an argument! "Great!" she said, hardly believing it. "I'll go and get some!"

"Daffodil!" Violet heard Ms Willow singing Daffodil's name as she came into the stable block. "Where are you, my sweetie? Come here!"

Daffodil tensed. "I've got to go."

Violet skipped to the store room and chose some red and gold ribbons. As she returned to Twinkle's stable, she saw Ms Willow stroking Daffodil.

"Hello, Violet." To Violet's relief, Ms Willow greeted her as if nothing had happened the night before. "How are you today? Has your cold quite gone?" Her eyes twinkled.

"Yes, thank you," said Violet sheepishly. She looked at the ribbon Ms Willow had in her hands. "That's a nice ribbon," she said, to change the subject. The ribbon was very unusual. It had a pearly sheen that was almost silver but not quite. It reminded Violet of something, but she couldn't remember what.

"I do like Daffodil to look pretty," said Ms Willow. "Right, time for your tonic, Daffodil, and then I'll get plaiting."

Violet returned to Twinkle's stable. But as she reached it, she stopped. An image of the scrap of material that Matilda had found in the secret room flashed into her head. The ribbon Ms Willow had been holding was the same silvery colour. Frowning, Violet went back to Daffodil's stable.

Ms Willow was just putting the tonic bottle down. She glanced round and asked, "Is everything all right, dear? You look worried."

"Yes, I just, er. . . I do really like that ribbon you have. Where did you get it from?"

"Just from the store room." Ms Willow held the ribbon up. "It's a lovely shade of purple, isn't it?"

Violet blinked. Purple? She'd been sure the ribbon was silver. But, no, the ribbon Ms Willow was holding was definitely a deep purple. Her eyes must be playing tricks on her.

"I'm sure you'll find some in the store room if

you look," said Ms Willow, smiling

"Thanks. I'll go and have a look later," said Violet and, feeling a bit foolish, she turned away.

"Matilda, have you got that piece of material we found in the secret room?" Violet asked later, as she got ready for afternoon lessons.

"Sure, it's somewhere round here." Matilda started to hunt around her bed, opening drawers. "Now, where did I put it?"

"You put it in here when we came down from the secret room," sighed Ariana, opening Matilda's jewellery box.

"Oh yes!" said Matilda. "Thanks." She handed it to Violet. "What do you want it for?"

"I just want to look at it." Violet turned the material from side to side. It had exactly the same silvery gleam as the ribbon that she was sure she had seen Ms Willow holding. *Why did I think Ms*

Willow's ribbon looked like this? Violet wondered. *Were my eyes playing tricks on me?*

"Are you OK?" Ariana asked.

"Yeah." But Violet felt something nagging at her. It wasn't just the ribbon. Something else was bothering her. What was it? Turning the scrap of material over in her hands, she realised. Daffodil! When Ms Willow had come into the stable, Daffodil had tensed up almost as though she was scared.

Violet almost laughed out loud. That was ridiculous! Everyone knew how much Ms Willow doted on Daffodil. She had to be mistaken.

I'll talk to Twinkle, she decided. *He's friends with Daffodil – he might have noticed something.* She'd ask him if he wanted to go on another night-time ride that night, and they could talk then. Happiness fizzed through her as she remembered how much fun they'd had on the first ride, until it had started snowing. It would be lovely to be out with him again. Just the two of them, in the peace of a starlit night.

It was cross-country that afternoon and Violet didn't have a chance to talk to Twinkle about going on a starlight ride until afterwards. As she filled his hay net, Twinkle left his stable to talk to Daffodil. They were whispering about something when Ms Willow came into the stable block. Daffodil gave Twinkle a quick nuzzle. "We'll speak more later, Twinkle," Violet heard her say softly, before she trotted over to join Ms Willow.

"What were you two talking about?" Violet asked curiously, as she and Twinkle went back to his stall.

"Just this and that," he said, shrugging.

Violet frowned. It wasn't like Twinkle to be

evasive. "What sort of this and that?"

Twinkle looked awkward. "Just unicorn stuff. You… You wouldn't understand."

Violet felt a stab of hurt. Whyever would he think she wouldn't understand? And what could he possibly have been talking about that he couldn't share with her? For a moment, she almost felt like she didn't want to go out for a ride that evening after all, but then she told herself not to be silly. She needed to talk to him, in private.

"I was thinking," she said, pushing her hurt aside. "How about we go for another starlight ride tonight?" She expected him to nod eagerly but, to her surprise, he looked worried.

"Tonight? No, I can't. Not tonight!"

Violet stared. "What? Why?"

"I… I don't want to. I'm… I'm… tired. Yes," he started yawning vigorously, "I'm very, very tired."

Violet frowned. "Twinkle, you're not tired."

"I am," insisted Twinkle, avoiding her gaze. "I really am."

Violet was dumbfounded. He was obviously lying about feeling tired, but why? Feeling hurt, and unsure of what to do, she tied up his hay net and picked up her coat. "OK, well, I'll see you in the morning then," she muttered.

"Wait, Violet!" A mixture of emotions swirled in Twinkle's eyes. "I can't meet you tonight, but

come and see me in the morning. Yes," he nodded determinedly. "In the morning, everything will be fine. Please come and talk to me then."

"OK," Violet said slowly. "I'll see you in the morning. Night, Twinkle." Frowning, she hurried away.

CHAPTER SEVEN

On the way back to school, all Violet could think about was Twinkle. Why was he being so secretive? And what had he meant when he said everything would be fine by the morning? Unease washed over her. It sounded like he was planning something – but what?

In the dining room, Diamond and Topaz dorms were sharing a table. Although dinner was her favourite, lasagne, Violet only picked at it. She couldn't leave things as they were with Twinkle. Even if it was difficult and awkward, she had to go back and talk to him. Clearing away

her half-empty plate, she slipped out. She put her coat and boots on and ran across the frosty lawn in the dark. As she got close to the stable block, Twinkle came out. Her heart lurched. Where was he off to?

"Twinkle!" Her voice sounded loud in the quiet night.

He froze guiltily.

"What are you doing?" she asked.

Twinkle avoided her eyes. "Um . . . going out. For… For a walk."

"At this time?" Violet forgot about not arguing with him – she'd had enough. She marched in front of Twinkle. "Stop lying to me!" she told him hotly. Twinkle's gaze flew to her face as she put her hands on her hips. "I mean it, Twinkle. I'm standing here until you tell me what's going on!" She was shaking with emotion. She didn't usually get angry, but this was too important, too big. She

had to know what Twinkle was up to. She waited for him to argue but, to her surprise, he hung his head.

"I'm meeting Daffodil," he muttered.

"What? Why?" said Violet in astonishment.

"She said she has something important to tell me, but she said we need to be outside in the starlight." Twinkle's dark eyes shone with excitement as he looked up. "Violet, I think it might be a way of speeding up the bonding process. Daffodil knows a lot about magic and she knows how much I want to bond with you. I think she might be able to help me."

Violet frowned. "But, Twinkle, Ms Rosemary said bonding happens when the time is right. If there was a way of speeding it up, then I'm sure she would have told us. There can't be anything Daffodil can do."

Twinkle looked stubborn. "But I think there

is. Why else would she say she had something important to talk to me about? I want to go and meet her, Violet."

Violet hesitated. Something didn't feel right. "Please let me go," he begged.

Violet didn't want to agree, but she also didn't want to upset him. "OK," she said reluctantly. "But I'm coming with you," she added.

"You don't need to," Twinkle began. "It's really cold out tonight."

"I don't care," said Violet. She gave him a firm look. "We either go to meet Daffodil together or you don't go at all, even if it means I have to stay in the stable with you all night."

She blinked. For a moment, she'd sounded a bit like Rosa! But it seemed to work.

Twinkle nodded. "All right. Let's go together. I'd rather you came with me anyway, but we'd better hurry or we'll be late. Daffodil said to meet

her at the edge of the woods."

Violet vaulted on to his back and they set off at a canter across the frosty lawn.

As they approached the woods, Violet saw a shadowy figure in a cloak moving across the grass ahead of them. She clutched Twinkle's mane and gasped. It was the hooded figure! But just then the moon came out from behind a cloud and showed

the person more clearly. Violet breathed a sigh of relief. No, it wasn't. It was just Ms Willow. "Did Daffodil tell you Ms Willow would be here too?" she said in surprise.

Twinkle slowed to a trot. A note of uncertainty crept into his voice as he replied, "No."

"Stop!" gasped Violet, suddenly spotting something on the ground. She stared in disbelief. A set of footprints tracked Ms Willow's progress across the frosty grass. Each footprint had a diamond-shaped pattern. "Twinkle! The footprints! They're just like the ones we found in the cave and in the secret room." An icy fear gripped her as Twinkle snorted in alarm and a horrible, almost unbelievable, thought struck her. Could Ms Willow be the cloaked figure who had been draining magic from the island?

CHAPTER EIGHT

"She's seen us!" Violet squeaked as Ms Willow swung round.

For a moment, she hoped she was mistaken, that Ms Willow was really just the lovely teacher she had always thought her to be, but as Ms Willow's face creased into a furious frown and her eyes hardened, Violet's heart sank into her boots.

"I knew something was going on!" Ms Willow's voice snapped out through the night air like an icicle cracking. "Trying to outsmart me!" She gave a shrill whistle and Daffodil emerged reluctantly from the trees. The little unicorn moved slowly,

almost as if she was fighting against leaving the woods but had no choice.

"Daffodil? You really should know better!" said Ms Willow. Daffodil sent Twinkle and Violet a desperate look but began to trot towards Ms Willow.

Violet didn't know what was going on, but she did know that she and Twinkle had to get help – and fast!

"Come on, Twinkle!" she gasped. "Let's get back to the school!"

Twinkle spun round and set off at a flat-out gallop just as Daffodil reached Ms Willow. Violet clung to his mane, her thoughts swirling. How could the cloaked figure be lovely Ms Willow? It just didn't seem possible. Something brushed past them at a great speed and suddenly Ms Willow and Daffodil appeared from nowhere, blocking their way. Twinkle had to swerve abruptly to avoid

crashing into them.

"There's no escape for you two now!" Ms
Willow hissed. Her voice sounded harsh
and bitter, nothing like her usual
soft tone. Before Twinkle or
Violet could do anything,
she flicked her hand.
There was a great
flash of green
and the world
tilted as Violet
and Twinkle spun
through the air.

Everything blurred.
Violet's hands numbed
as she desperately hung on
to Twinkle's neck. Then they were
falling. Violet tensed, expecting the worst, but
Twinkle's hooves sunk into the ground and he

landed with a bounce as the world came back into focus.

Above them, the inky night sky glittered with thousands of stars. Their light was reflected by the thick ice of a huge frozen lake, and Violet realised that they were standing just at its edge. At the far side, a strip of land separated it from a vast black sea. Beneath the layer of ice, the water looked dark.

"Where are we?" said Twinkle.

"I think it's the Frozen Lagoon!" breathed Violet. "We learnt about it from Ms Rivers a month ago. It's bottomless, it's always frozen, and supposedly no one's ever been able to find it because magic keeps its location secret."

A thin mist swirled like ghosts above the dark ice. Beneath it, they could see the water bubbling like a volcano on the verge of eruption. Violet shivered – there was something unnatural about

the way the mist was moving and the sickly sweet smell was rising from it that scared her.

"Why do you think Ms Willow brought us here?" said Twinkle.

"I don't know," said Violet. "I can't believe she's the cloaked figure, Twinkle. She's always seemed so nice."

"I can't believe that Daffodil has been helping her," said Twinkle, shaking his head in astonishment.

"I don't understand. Whenever we saw the cloaked figure with a unicorn, it didn't look anything like Daffodil," said Violet. "It was taller, with a long golden mane, just like Prancer, the stolen unicorn. It didn't look anything like Daffodil."

"Maybe Ms Willow has two unicorns," suggested Twinkle.

It seemed the only explanation. Violet looked

around. "What are we going to do now?"

"Try and escape?" suggested Twinkle.

There was a flash of green and Ms Willow and Daffodil landed nearby.

Twinkle reared bravely, slashing the air with his forelegs. Then, wheeling around, he galloped away. Ms Willow's laughter echoed after him.

"You can run but there's no escape from me!"

Violet ducked as something whizzed over her head. A bolt of magic hit the rocks in front of them, which exploded into shards. Twinkle swerved, and the sour smell of bad magic filled Violet's nostrils.

"Don't try and get away – you'll only get hurt," Daffodil called anxiously.

Twinkle swung round. "Daffodil, why are you helping her? I thought you were my friend!"

Ms Willow smirked. "Oh, dear sweet Daffodil has no choice! Those ribbons – the ones you

admired so much, Violet – contain a powerful binding spell and, while they are in her mane, Daffodil must obey my every command. For some reason, she thought that she could warn you tonight about what was going on, but she should have known better. I have forbidden her to speak of my plans so, even if she had met with you, she couldn't have told you anything."

Daffodil gave Twinkle a desperate look. "I thought I would find a way and..." she gasped and fell silent as Ms Willow glared at her.

"Let us go!" Violet cried.

"What?" sneered Ms Willow. "And have you return to school and tell everyone about me? I think not. You will stay here while I see out my scheme to force every unicorn on Unicorn Island to do my bidding. I have spent years preparing for this. I am not going to let one foolish girl and her unicorn, who hasn't even found his magic, stop

me." She dismounted. "Daffodil – lock them up!"

Daffodil reluctantly trotted over to Twinkle and Violet and started to herd them towards a stone hut, her sharp horn digging into their backs.

"My friends will wonder where I am. They'll try and find me!" Violet shouted defiantly.

Ms Willow's eyes narrowed. "Hmm, you may be right. They have interfered before – sticking their noses in where they are not wanted. I'll deal

with them, too."

Violet caught her breath. "What do you mean? What—"

Ms Willow clicked her fingers and the door to the hut flew open.

Twinkle swung round and charged at Daffodil, but Ms Willow sent a bolt of green magic from her fingertips. It flew straight at him and Violet, knocking them off their feet and sending them flying backwards. As they tumbled into the hut, the heavy wooden door slammed shut and the bolts shot across. They were trapped!

CHAPTER NINE

Violet thumped her fists against the door and Twinkle battered it with his hooves, but it held firm. Eventually, they sank back, exhausted.

"What are we going to do?" Violet said in despair. "We've got to get out of here and warn the others. If Ms Willow captures them, it'll be all our fault." She threw her arms around his neck.

Twinkle nuzzled her. "I'm sorry, Violet. I got us into this mess. I shouldn't have insisted on meeting Daffodil."

Violet shook her head. "I agreed to go with you. But I wonder why she asked you to meet her.

It sounds like she wouldn't have been able to tell you anything about Ms Willow's plans anyway."

"I don't know," said Twinkle. "She just said she wanted to meet me somewhere outside in the starlight to tell me something important, but that doesn't matter now. We need to try and get out of here." He pawed at the earth with a front hoof. "Maybe we could dig our way out."

The sudden sound of voices and whinnies outside the hut made Violet shudder. "Twinkle, we're too late!" she gasped.

"Where are we? Why have you brought us here?" she heard Rosa shout angrily.

"Let us go!" exclaimed Matilda.

"So you can ruin my plans, you annoying girls? Never!" Ms Willow sneered. "I warned you about snooping around the school at night. You should have stayed in your dorm!"

"We were looking for Violet. She's missing."

Ariana sounded close to tears.

"I'm in here, with Twinkle!" Violet yelled, hammering on the door.

"Violet!" yelled Freya. "Help me, everyone. Let's get her out!"

"CHARGE!" Rosa shouted.

Violet's heart leapt as she heard the thunder of hooves. Ms Willow shrieked, and suddenly the bolts of the hut door grated and it swung open. Violet could hardly believe her eyes. Rosa, Matilda and Ariana, riding their unicorns, had clearly charged at Ms Willow, cornering her at the edge of the frozen lagoon. She was lying on the ground. Meanwhile, Freya must have used Honey's superspeed to reach the hut and pull the bolts back.

"We're free!" gasped Twinkle, as he cantered out.

Violet saw Ms Willow raise her hands. "Watch

out!" she cried, guessing what she was about to do.

Three fiery bolts of green magic shot at Crystal, Whisper and Pearl's legs, sending them and the girls tumbling on to the ice. In the chaos of shouts and whinnies, Ms Willow scrambled to her feet and sent another two bolts of magic flying towards Freya and Violet.

Honey used her superspeed to get Freya to safety. Violet smelt a faint scent of burnt sugar but the next moment she felt Twinkle barrelling into her, knocking her to the ground. The green bolts of magic flashed past her head, burning through the ends of his mane. They hit the back wall of the hut, exploding in a shower of sparks that stung like needles as they hit Violet's face. There was no time to waste. Leaping up, Violet threw herself on to Twinkle's back. Freya and Honey were already at the lagoon, slithering on to the ice to help the others get to their feet.

Twinkle raced to join them.

Ms Willow hurled more firebolts at the girls and their unicorns. Hissing and spitting, the magical bolts cut through the ice like a laser, melting a circle around them.

"We're going to fall in!" cried Ariana, as the circle of ice they were standing on began to sink.

"We're not – Crystal can save us," gasped Rosa. "Use your freezing powers, Crystal!"

A cloud of pink sparks swirled around Crystal as she refroze the ice around them as fast as it melted.

"No, you don't!" Ms Willow aimed a firebolt straight at Crystal's head.

"Crystal!" screamed Rosa.

"Pearl – help her!" The next second, a swirling tornado of snow rose up around Crystal, hiding her from sight. With a frustrated cry, Ms Willow threw the firebolt blindly at the snowstorm, where

it flew harmlessly past Rosa and Crystal.

Fast and furious, Ms Willow threw more firebolts, but Pearl made the snow twister illusion bigger until all the girls and their unicorns were hidden behind it. The firebolts flashed by, exploding with ferocious bangs far behind them.

Meanwhile, Whisper started to use his magic. Skating to the edge of the snowstorm, he focused his attention on Daffodil until the little unicorn began to relax and sway.

"Pull yourself together, you stupid thing!" screamed Ms Willow as Daffodil rocked on her hooves beneath her.

"Whisper! That's brilliant! Don't stop!" said Ariana as Whisper kept using his soothing magic on Daffodil. The little unicorn's eyes started to close and her knees began to give way. For a moment, it looked like she was about to fall asleep completely, but then Whisper began to tire. Doing

magic used up a lot of energy.

Ms Willow kicked Daffodil's sides viciously. "Get back on your feet this instant!" she snarled.

With Whisper's magic fading, Daffodil obeyed Ms Willow's command, raising her head and straightening her neck.

"Matilda!" Pearl gasped, breathing heavily. "I can't hold the glamour. I'm. . . I'm too tired."

The snow twister faded, revealing everyone to Ms Willow. She stood before them, her eyes wild and her hair crackling with magic. Triumph lit up her cold eyes. "Now you shall all suffer for the trouble you have caused me!" She raised her hands to blast them.

"No! You're not going to hurt my friends!" whinnied Twinkle bravely. He charged at her, but his hooves slipped on the treacherous ice and he fell over. Violet was flung from his back. The island's protective magic made a bubble form

around her and it set her gently down on the ice before popping.

Twinkle struggled to his feet just as Ms Willow threw a bolt of magic straight at his heart. "Twinkle!" Violet exclaimed. She leapt in front of him.

"Violet!" she heard Rosa yell in horror.

Violet and Twinkle

Violet shut her eyes, waiting for the bolt to hit her, but instead she just saw a flash of light through her closed eyelids. Her friends squealed and Violet smelt burnt sugar. Blinking her eyes open, she was astonished to see that the air in front of her was shimmering as it bent around her and the others like an enormous transparent shield!

"What. . . What's happening?" said Twinkle in shock.

"It's your magic!" cried Violet. "It must be!"

Ms Willow screamed with rage. Dismounting from Daffodil, she strode to the edge of the lagoon, her eyes fixed on the magic shield. While her attention was diverted, Daffodil saw her chance. She galloped past Ms Willow and dived behind the shield with the others. Instantly, she grew taller, and her yellow and orange colouring faded to be replaced by a splendid golden mane and tail.

"It's Prancer!" cried Matilda.

"You can use starlight to make a protective shield, Twinkle!" Prancer gasped. "I guessed you had starlight magic when you told me about your night-time ride with Violet, and how the snow stopped falling on you for a moment when you wanted to protect her."

Twinkle whinnied in delight just as Ms Willow shrieked, "Prancer! Return to me this instant! I command it!"

Violet expected Prancer to obey, but the unicorn didn't. Her eyes shone. "This is why I wanted to meet you in the starlight tonight, Twinkle!" she rushed on. "I hoped this would happen. When I'm protected by your starlight magic, the binding ribbons don't work and I can reveal my true form and speak freely. I've been desperate to tell someone what's been happening. I've been wanting to warn people how evil Ms Willow really is."

Twinkle's sides heaved as Ms Willow threw firebolt after firebolt at the shield. "This is hard work! I don't know how long I can hold it," he panted.

Prancer looked at the others. "You need to escape and warn everyone about Ms Willow. She's been stealing all the island's magic and storing it here in the lagoon so that she can take over the island." Ms Willow's firebolts continued to batter at the shield. "She's held a grudge against the unicorns ever since she didn't get a place at the academy when she was younger. She vowed she would use magic anyway and spent years learning dark magic, then she stole me from my home so that she could use my spell-weaving powers. She put binding ribbons in my mane and commanded me to disguise myself. You have to stop her. She has an evil plan to put all the unicorns on the island under her command. She—"

"I can't hold the shield any longer!" Twinkle interrupted, sinking to his knees.

"Twinkle!" cried Violet, throwing herself down beside him. "Keep trying."

But the shield wavered and Ms Willow screamed with delight as a bolt of magic tore through the top of it.

"You must leave now!" insisted Prancer.

"Crystal, take everyone back to school in a snow twister. Tell everyone there what is going on. I'll hold Ms Willow off. She must be stopped!"

"But what about you, Prancer?" cried Violet.

Two bolts ripped through the shield. "Don't worry about me. Just go!"

Crystal stamped her front hooves. Pink and purple sparkles swirled up from the ice and surrounded the girls and their unicorns in a glowing cloud, as a snow twister rose around them. Faster it whirled, whisking the girls and their unicorns into the air as Twinkle's starlight shield split into millions of sparkling pieces. Violet sighed in relief as they spun away, with Ms Willow's furious screams echoing in their ears.

CHAPTER TEN

Violet felt her feet hit grass and, as the sparkles cleared, she saw the turrets of Unicorn Academy and heard her friends and their unicorns all talking at once. Crystal's snow twister had brought them to the lawn outside the school. Crystal hung her head, taking deep breaths, and Twinkle dropped to the ground, exhausted.

"We need to get the teachers straight away!" said Matilda.

"You all go!" Violet told them. "The unicorns need sky berries to help them recover."

"We can get some, can't we, Rosa? I feel stronger

already," said Crystal, who was more used to using her magic than the others. Rosa nodded and the pair left for the stables while the others galloped off to rouse the teachers.

"I'm sorry, I didn't have enough energy to hold the shield any longer," Twinkle said to Violet, his sides heaving. "I hope Prancer is OK."

"Me too. It must be horrible being under the command of someone like Ms Willow, but now we know we'll be able to try and help free her. You were amazing, Twinkle. You saved us all and held the shield long enough for Prancer to tell us what's going on." Violet threw her arms round his neck. "I'm so proud of you."

Twinkle nuzzled her. "I wouldn't have found my magic if you hadn't jumped in front of me to protect me from Ms Willow. I thought you were going to be hurt. It was really brave of you. You shouldn't have done it though. I'm meant to

protect you."

"No, that's wrong!" Violet said hotly.

He looked at her. "We protect each other, Twinkle," she told him, more gently. "We're a team. It's not just you protecting me. We're partners."

"Partners," he said slowly, as if getting his head around the idea.

Violet smiled. "Yes. So, from now on, no more thinking you are the only one who has to do the protecting. And," she took a deep breath – she didn't want to ruin the moment but she knew that now was the right time to say something – "no more bossing me around all the time, OK?"

"What do you mean?" said Twinkle in surprise.

"You keep making decisions for both of us without asking what I want," Violet told him.

Twinkle thought about it. "I suppose I do." He looked at her through his eyelashes. "But if you don't want me to do that then you need to tell me

what it is that you want, Violet. I can't be a mind reader."

Violet realised he was right. She'd spent so much time thinking about how bossy he was, but really she was as much to blame for not speaking out. She needed to stop always agreeing with him and make sure she told him what her opinion was. "Agreed," she said firmly. "From now on, we'll make decisions together. We'll be a real team."

He snorted happily. "I'd like that."

Rosa came cantering back with a bucket of sky berries. She jumped off Crystal then shared the sky berries out. "Here you go, Twinkle. Eat these and you'll soon feel better. Oh, my goodness!" She broke off with a gasp. "You've bonded!"

Violet lifted her plait and saw a strand of purple and blue hair running through it. "We have! Look, Twinkle!"

Twinkle's eyes sparkled in delight. "We're going

to graduate after all, Violet." She flung her arms round him and hugged him tightly.

"Violet! Matilda!" Ms Nettles came hurrying across the grass with Ms Rosemary.

Rosa, Ariana and Freya followed them. "Are you and your unicorns all right?"

They nodded.

Looks of relief crossed the teachers' faces.

"I can hardly believe Ms Willow is behind

all this," said Ms Rosemary. She turned to Ms Nettles. "What are we going to do?"

"We must find her and stop her," said Ms Nettles. "We must also free poor Prancer of the binding."

"We'll help," offered Rosa.

Ms Nettles' strict face relaxed into a small smile. "I think you've all done quite enough for now," she said. "Thank you, Diamond dorm. You've been very brave. Now, take your unicorns back to the stables and then off to bed, all of you. I'll arrange for some hot chocolate and cookies to be sent up to your dorm for when you get back."

"Something tells me Ms Willow won't allow herself to be caught that easily," said Freya, as Twinkle finished the sky berries and stood up, his strength restored.

"I wonder what she's planning on doing," said Ariana uneasily, as Violet vaulted on to Twinkle's

back. "How is she going to control all the unicorns?"

"I don't know," said Rosa. "But Ms Nettles is right, she has to be stopped. And if there's any way we can help, we will!"

"Hooray for Diamond dorm!" whooped Matilda and the others joined in the cheer.

They raced back to the stable block but, as the others headed inside, Twinkle held back and looked up at the glittering sky. "I always said I liked the starlight, didn't I?" he said softly to Violet.

"You did. You said it gave you a magical feeling," said Violet. "I guess we just didn't know how true that was!" She smiled. "Starlight magic is so cool. We'll have to go for lots of night-time rides from now on so you can practise it."

Twinkle turned and looked at her. "One little canter before bedtime, now I've got my energy back?"

Violet grinned. "Yes, let's!"

With a happy toss of his head, Twinkle set off

across the frosty grass. As the cold air stung Violet's
cheeks, she buried her hands in his long mane and
urged him faster as the bright stars twinkled down at
them from the clear night sky.

PRINCESS of PETS

Look out for a BRILLIANT new
Nosy Crow series from the author
of The Rescue Princesses!

Animal adventures,
friendship and a royal family!